Usborne Flip-Flaps
What happens to your food?

Alastair Smith

Illustrated by Maria Wheatley

Designed by Maria Wheatley and Ruth Russell

Digital artwork by John Russell

Series editor: Judy Tatchell

What is food for?

Without food, your body would stop working, like a car that has run out of fuel.

Food gives you energy to move around.

Food makes you grow bigger.

Food helps you stay strong and healthy.

Feeling hungry

When you are hungry, your stomach feels empty. It might make rumbling noises.

If you don't eat, the feeling of hunger grows and grows.

He needs food!

You might start to feel floppy and unhappy.

Your food's journey

After you swallow your food, it goes down a long, wiggly tube inside you.

The food slides down the wiggly food tube. It is broken up into tiny pieces.

Your body uses the tiny pieces to keep you going.

Food slides down here.

Your food tube looks a little like a pile of uncooked sausages. It is all curled up inside you.

If your food tube were pulled out straight it would be about four times as long as you.

This is what your food tube would look like, pulled out straight.

This is your stomach. It is part of your food tube.

This part of your food tube is all curled up.

The hole in your bottom is called your anus.

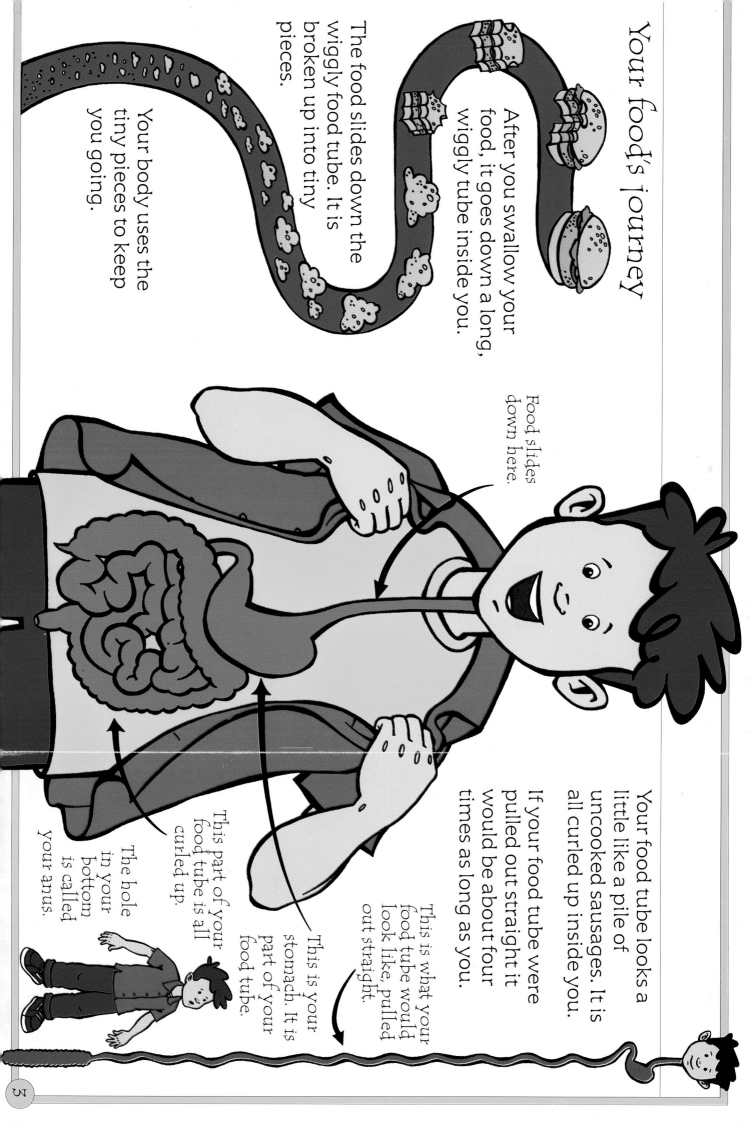

3

What should you eat?

You need to eat different kinds of food. This keeps your body healthy.

Some foods are good for helping you to grow. They also help to mend cuts and bruises. Here are some of them.

Potatoes

Bread

Pasta

Beans

Rice

Milk

Cheese

Fish

Some kinds of food are very good for giving you energy. You can see some of these above.

Your body needs vitamins and minerals. These keep it working well. Fruit and vegetables have lots of these.

Apples

Oranges

Eggs

Lettuce

Carrots

Strawberries

Tomatoes

Just take a look inside!

The food tube starts at your mouth.

The food tube ends at the hole in your bottom.

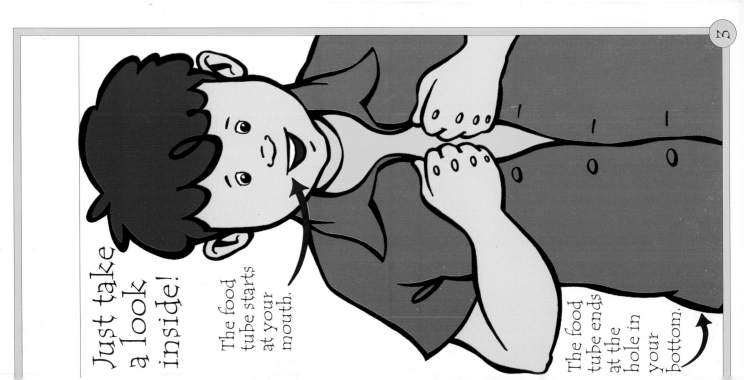

What shouldn't you eat?

You shouldn't eat things that have gone bad. Food goes bad when it gets old.

Also, beware of germs in food.

What are germs?

Germs are tiny creatures. They are too small for you to see. Some germs can make you ill if you eat them.

Making germs really hot is a good way to kill them. That's why you should cook meat and fish.

You don't have to cook fruit and vegetables to get rid of germs. Just wash them well before you eat them.

Is it yummy?

How do you decide what you want to eat?

Look at it...
You decide whether you like the look of it.

Yuck!

Yum!

Smell it...
You decide whether you like the way it smells.

Remember it...
You remember what you thought of it last time you tasted it.

Taste it...
You decide whether you like the way it tastes.

How can you get rid of germs?

Be a germ killer...

We love to live in meat and fish.

Please don't lift the flap!

Making food yummy

You can mix things together and cook them to make great new tastes.

Different parts of your tongue taste different things.

Even making food look nice can help you to enjoy it.

Sauces or dressings can make things taste more interesting.

sweet

salty

sour

salty

sour

bitter

Sweet things taste sweetest on the tip of your tongue.

Your tongue can taste sweet things, salty things, sour things and bitter things.

What happens in your mouth?

About your teeth

You have different types of teeth. They do different jobs.

Sharp cutter teeth cut food up.

Bumpy teeth grind and chew.

Pointed teeth tear food into shreds.

Your mouth is a food masher. It changes the things you eat into a slippery paste. This paste is easy to swallow.

Your teeth chop your food up into little pieces.

Your tongue pushes the food around inside your mouth.

Spit makes food soft and slippery. It slides down your throat.

Taste test

How do you taste different things?

How many teeth?

Newborn babies have no teeth. You grow your first teeth when you are a few months old. You grow 20 baby teeth.

Your baby teeth start to fall out when you are about six. You grow 32 bigger teeth instead. These should last all your life.

Taking a bite

First you open wide, then ...

... Crunch! Chew! Chop!

Teeth

Spit is made here.

Windpipe

Tongue

Ball of food

Swallowing

Your tongue rolls chewed food into a ball. It pushes the ball to the back of your mouth.

You swallow and the food goes down your food tube.

Why do you choke?

Air goes down your windpipe when you breathe. Sometimes, food goes down the wrong way, into your windpipe. You choke to get the food out.

This ball of food is starting its journey through the food tube.

Into your stomach

Your food's next stop on its way down the food tube is in your stomach. This is like a squashy bag.

Where is your stomach?

Your stomach is about level with your elbows.

What does your stomach do?

Your stomach squeezes and mashes food up. It pours special stomach juices on the food. These help mush it up. It ends up like a slushy soup.

Food plops into your stomach here.

Stomach juices

Stomach

Food squirts out of your stomach here.

How big is your stomach?

If your stomach is empty it is about as big as this picture of a balloon. But your stomach can stretch to hold a big meal.

A grown-up's empty stomach is about twice as big as this picture of a balloon.

Eating too much

Sometimes you eat and drink too much. Your stomach might decide that it's had enough.

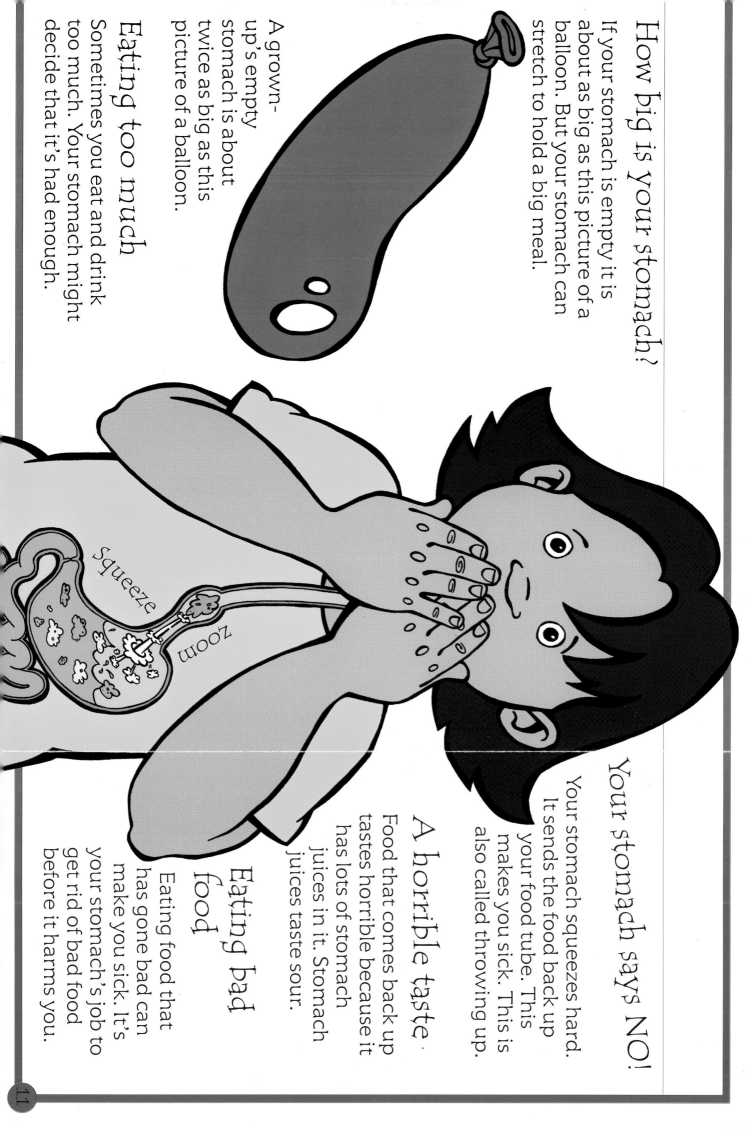

squeeze

zoom

Your stomach says NO!

Your stomach squeezes hard. It sends the food back up your food tube. This makes you sick. This is also called throwing up.

A horrible taste

Food that comes back up tastes horrible because it has lots of stomach juices in it. Stomach juices taste sour.

Eating bad food

Eating food that has gone bad can make you sick. It's your stomach's job to get rid of bad food before it harms you.

Where food goes next

What's that noise?

After a meal you may hear gurgling noises coming from inside you. What's going on?

Bash

Mash

Gurgle

Don't worry, it's only your food being mashed and squeezed in your food tube.

The slushy food gets out of your stomach through a small hole. It squirts through the hole little by little.

Now it goes into a long, curled-up part of the food tube. This is your small intestine.

Moving along

The food tube squeezes food along all the way from your mouth to your anus.

It works like toothpaste being squeezed up a tube.

What happens next?

In the small intestine

Here, special juices, called digestive juices, squirt onto the food. These dissolve the food pieces into even tinier pieces.

Digestive juices

Digestive juices turn the food into smaller pieces.

Small intestine

Tiny food pieces are sucked out through the sides of the tube. They travel around your body in your blood to where they are needed.

Digestive juices turn the food into smaller pieces.

Stomach

Hole open. Food squirts out.

There is still some leftover food in the small intestine. It is watery and sloppy by now.

This sloppy stuff is on its way to the next part of the food tube.

Journey's end

At the end of your small intestine, food is squeezed into the next part of the food tube. This is called the large intestine.

What happens here?

The large intestine works like a sieve. It sucks water out of the sloppy food through its sides.

The food left behind gets more solid and sludgy as water drains out.

The large intestine is wider and shorter than the small intestine.

The large intestine ends at your anus.

Water comes out through the sides.

Sloppy food

Stomach

The hole opens and closes to let food through. Here it is closed.

Where do the food pieces go next?

Let's get out of here!

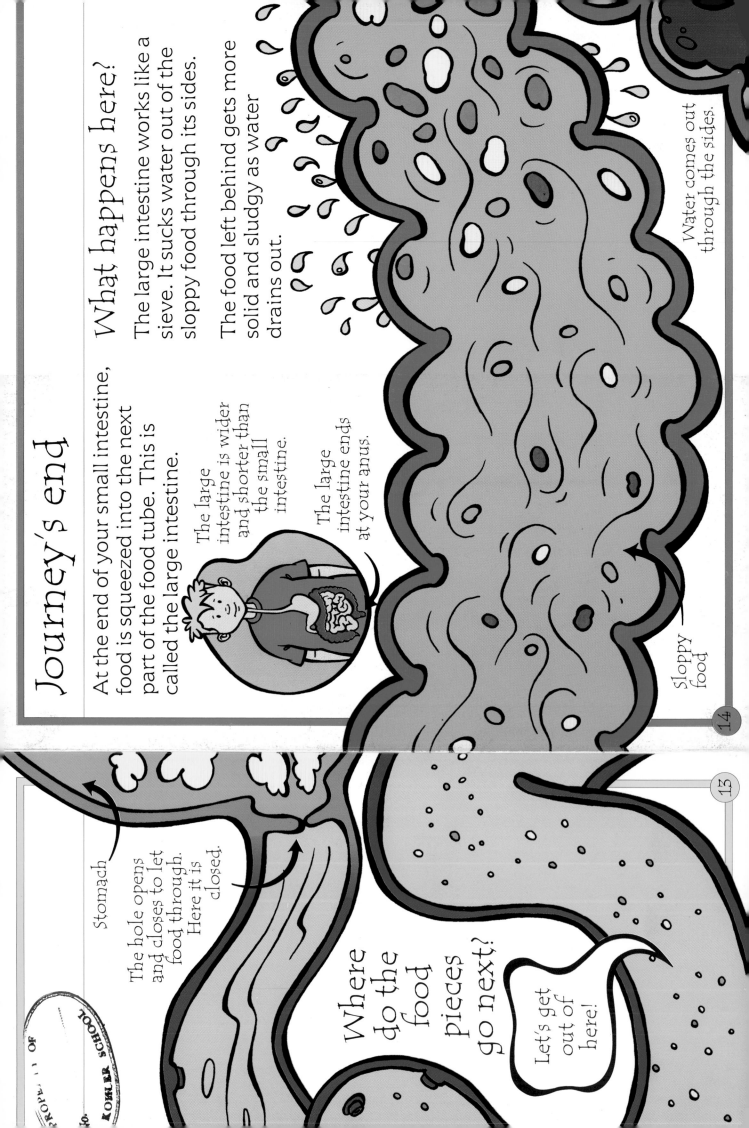

What's in the sludgy stuff?

The sludgy stuff is mostly food your body cannot use.

There's still a little water left in the sludgy stuff. This helps it to slip and slide along.

This food isn't sloppy any more. It is soft and sludgy.

What happens then?

Let's go to the bathroom...

You let the sludgy stuff out of your body about once a day, on the toilet.

A slow journey

The food you eat can take up to three days to slide all the way through your food tube. It's a long, slow journey!

This is the end of the journey

Index

anus 3, 14

bad food 5, 11
blood 13
bottom 3

choking 9

digestive juices 12, 13

eating too much 11

food tube 3, 9, 10, 12, 14, 15

germs 5

hunger 2

large intestine 14

mouth 3, 8, 9

sick, being 11
small intestine 12, 13, 14
spit 8, 9
stomach 2, 3, 10, 11, 12, 13
stomach juices 10, 11
swallowing 9

tasting 6, 7
teeth 8, 9
throwing up 11
toilet, going to the 15
tongue 7, 8

water 14, 15
windpipe 9

First published in 1997 by Usborne Publishing Ltd, Usborne House, 83-85 Saffron Hill, London, EC1N 8RT, England. www.usborne.com Copyright © 2003, 1997 Usborne Publishing Ltd.

The name Usborne and the devices ⊕ ⊜ are the Trade Marks of Usborne Publishing Ltd. All rights reserved. No part of this publication may be reproduced, stored in a retrieval system or transmitted in any form or by any means, electronic, mechanical, photocopying, recording or otherwise, without the prior permission of the publisher. Printed in Italy.

First published in America August 1997 UE

Bathroom

MORE STORIES IN PAPERBACK FROM FRANCES LINCOLN CHILDREN'S BOOKS

The Leopard's Drum
An Asante tale from West Africa

Jessica Souhami

Osebo the leopard has a fine, huge, magnificent drum,
but he won't let anyone else play it - not even Nyame, the Sky-God.
So Nyame offers a big reward to the animal who will bring him the drum...
How a very small tortoise outwits the boastful leopard is dramatically
retold in this traditional tale from West Africa.

ISBN 978-0-7112-0907-3 (UK)
ISBN 978-1-84507-506-4 (US)

The King With Horse's Ears

Eric Maddern

Illustrated by Paul Hess

No one knows about King Mark's ears except his barber.
Keeping the secret eventually drives him to the doctor,
who advises him to whisper it to the ground.
But sooner or later, truth will out . . . .

ISBN 978-0-7112-2079-9 (UK)
ISBN 978-1-84507-309-1 (US)